AF559678

The Platoon under the Moon

Books by Delshad Karanjia

Teaching a Horse to Sing: Tales of Uncommon Sense from India and Elsewhere

Akbar and Birbal: The Finest Stories of the Emperor and His Wise Minister

The Platoon under the Moon

SIX TALES OF MULLAH NASRUDDIN

DELSHAD KARANJIA

Illustrations by Mohit Suneja

ALEPH

ALEPH BOOK COMPANY
An independent publishing firm
promoted by ***Rupa Publications India***

First published in India in 2025
by Aleph Book Company
7/16 Ansari Road, Daryaganj
New Delhi 110 002

This is a work of fiction. Names, characters, places, and incidents are either the product of the author's imagination or are used fictitiously and any resemblance to any actual persons, living or dead, events, or locales is entirely coincidental.

ISBN: 978-93-6523-325-4

1 3 5 7 9 10 8 6 4 2

Printed in India

In a Class of His Own

For Nasruddin and his classmates, school was an unnecessary evil, given that none of them wanted to be scholars, with most of them likely to become farmers or take up the family trade. With schoolmaster Halil completely failing to inspire a passion for learning in his students, they were always looking for opportunities to play truant.

One day, Halil entered the classroom carrying three glass jars containing fruit sweets and plonked them on his desk. 'Boys,' he announced, 'all the sweets in these jars will be yours if you can answer a simple arithmetic question. There are forty sweets distributed amongst these three jars. The first jar contains seven more sweets than the second jar. The third jar has three less sweets than the second jar. Can you calculate how many sweets there are in the first jar?'

Getting nothing but vacant stares and stifled yawns from his unresponsive students, Halil slowly repeated the question, but no one wanted to calculate how many sweets the first jar contained.

'Wouldn't it be quicker to empty the first jar and count the number of sweets?' muttered Nasruddin, eliciting audible approval from his uninterested classmates.

Clutching his head in despair, Halil declared: 'Shameless and impertinent boys! You are all completely incapable of acquiring knowledge or bettering yourselves. I don't know why your parents are wasting my time by sending you donkeys to school. You would be better off grazing in the fields outside with your four-legged brethren.'

This was just the excuse Nasruddin needed: 'You are right, sir! We would indeed be better off in the fields,' and turning to his classmates he said:

'Come on, let's go and join our four-legged relatives as our esteemed teacher advises.' With shouts of delight, following Nasruddin's lead, the boys raced out of the classroom, holding on to their fezzes as they ran whooping and braying across the fields to their homes.

Surprised to see Nasruddin back from school so early, Leyla asked what had happened. Her son narrated an edited version of the morning's events, omitting all mention of the unsolved arithmetic problem that had triggered the schoolmaster's tirade and his own role in leading the raucous exodus from the class.

'Your teacher was wrong to call a

clever boy like you a donkey!' said Leyla, giving her son a hug. 'He needs to learn that even donkeys respond better if they're tempted with carrots instead of threatened with sticks.'

At school the next morning, the boys were somewhat subdued, expecting some form of punishment for leaving the classroom so unashamedly the day before, but were surprised that their teacher made no mention of the incident. Instead, Halil continued his mission to engage his unruly class in learning simple arithmetic. 'Boys, if you bought one onion, one cabbage, three tomatoes, two potatoes, and three carrots, how many vegetables would you have?' he intoned slowly and carefully, holding up the corresponding number of fingers for each vegetable to make things easier for his dull students.

Surprised to see his most difficult student raise a hand, Halil beamed: 'Nasruddin, please tell the class how many vegetables you have bought.'

'Enough to make a tasty soup,' came the reply.

Free Choice

A new bakery opened up in Nasruddin's home town Aksehir, on the same road that Nasruddin and his classmates took on their way to and from school. The aroma of freshly baked bread, pastries, and other delicacies enticed the boys although none of them had any money to buy the tempting goodies.

To attract new customers, the bakery put up a large sign: TRY OUR HOMEMADE BAKLAVA. THE BEST IN TOWN. FRESHLY PREPARED EVERY THURSDAY. FREE SAMPLES AVAILABLE.

Nasruddin and four of his friends went into the shop and asked to try the free samples. The kind baker placed a tray of baklava on the counter but before he could say 'help yourselves', five grubby hands had grabbed fistfuls of the sweetmeat and emptied the tray.

'Thank you,' they called out in muffled, chuckling voices as they scampered out

of the shop with their mouths crammed full.

The next Thursday, the boys headed for the bakery but found that the sign had been modified. It now read: TRY OUR HOMEMADE BAKLAVA. THE BEST IN TOWN. FRESHLY PREPARED EVERY THURSDAY.

'Can we have free samples of the baklava, please?' the boys asked the baker eagerly.

'We don't give free samples any more,' he replied, shooing them out like flies.

Every Thursday, for three weeks in a row, Nasruddin and his friends unfailingly stopped by the bakery asking for free samples, and got the same negative reply. On the fourth Thursday, when the boys appeared and asked for free samples, the baker lost his temper.

'I've told you repeatedly that we don't offer free samples of baklava any more. If I see you boys in my shop again next week asking for free samples, I will chase you out with a cane and then whip you on the street.'

The following Thursday, Nasruddin, with his pals in tow, went up to the bakery and asked: 'Do you have a cane and a whip?'

'No, I don't,' the baker replied, frowning.

'That's good,' Nasruddin smiled. 'Do you have any free samples of baklava?'

Nasruddin the Brave

A group of soldiers passing through Aksehir on their way to join their platoon stopped off at the teahouse and started bragging about their exploits in combat. Finding in the villagers a receptive and trusting audience, the soldiers' boasts about their heroic feats became

more and more audacious.

A tall and muscular trooper twirled his impressive moustache and proclaimed: 'Even though we were outnumbered two to one, the enemy did not stand a chance against my platoon. With sword in hand, we charged towards them fearlessly, wielding our blades left, right, and centre until the majority of our opponents were decimated and a handful of them beat a hasty retreat, scattering like chickens in a barn escaping a fox.'

His awe-stricken audience burst into applause amid cries of 'Bravo!'

Unable to tolerate other people bragging, Mullah Nasruddin cleared his throat and said: 'Your bravery reminds me of the time when I was caught up in a fierce battle.' The local teashop's regular customers looked at each other in surprise, never having known their mullah to have been anywhere near the front lines, as he added dramatically: 'The enemy soldiers were charging towards us, brandishing their swords in the air. When I was close enough to one of them, I gripped my sword firmly in both hands and with a downward swipe I cut off his arm. Chopped it off with one clean blow.'

'When it comes to dealing with an enemy, sir, it would have been better if you had cut off the enemy's head,' said the captain of the soldiers.

‘That was actually my intention,’ Nasruddin nodded, ‘but I found that somebody had already taken care of that.’

Before anyone could question his heroism, Nasruddin continued: ‘On another occasion, some years ago, I came to the rescue of an entire platoon. I was passing by a field where our king’s soldiers were resting after a fierce battle in which they had slaughtered the enemy. As I knew the commanding officer and many of the soldiers, they asked for my assistance. Several of the men had been severely wounded and needed medical help.

‘Their commanding officer requested me to ride back into town and ask the authorities to send doctors and medical supplies for the injured soldiers. Being a local and familiar with the terrain, he was sure I would be able to pinpoint their location,' Nasruddin said, pausing dramatically for a sip of tea.

'Did help reach them in time?' a soldier asked.

'Yes, eventually,' Nasruddin replied. 'The rescue party seemed to have some difficulty finding the platoon even though I had specified that the camp site was located directly under the moon.'

The Mullah's Fall

Nasruddin was on his way to the bazaar, riding his donkey facing backwards, as usual, and fantasizing about expanding his business and buying a bigger house, when a group of young boys lit fireworks in the middle of the market square. Startled by the loud explosions, Akilli took off like a racehorse, causing the daydreaming mullah to violently jerk backwards and almost fall off, his turban slipping forward over his eyes and blinding him.

Trying desperately to get Akilli to stop, Nasruddin grabbed on to her tail with both hands, but the frightened animal continued her frenzied gallop around the marketplace, causing shoppers to run helter-skelter to get out of her way.

'Where are you going in such a hurry, Mullah?' one of the vendors called out.

'Don't ask me, ask my donkey,' Nasruddin gasped, sliding from side to side on Akilli's back as he struggled to sit up straight.

When Akilli slowed down to a trot

after several laps round the market, Nasruddin let go of her tail with one hand to readjust his turban, but lost his balance and slipped off the donkey's back, knocking over a basket of peaches as he fell to the ground with a thud. Mayhem ensued as a few passers-by grabbed hold of the mullah's arms to help him to sit up, the fruit seller scuttled about trying to salvage any fruit that had not been crushed under the mullah's weight, Akilli scampered off to a safe distance, and the boys who had sparked the fireworks doubled over with laughter at the sight of the mullah sprawled on his back, his turban muddied, and his tunic stained with peach juice.

Struggling back to his feet, embarrassed at the spectacle he'd made of himself, Nasruddin faced his young tormentors and asked them angrily: 'What are you laughing at, you foolish boys? Does it not occur to you that I might have wanted to get off my donkey anyway?'

Dressing for a Feast

Hearing that an iftar banquet was being held at the home of the wealthiest man in town, to which everyone was invited, Nasruddin made his way to the feast after a full day's work on his farm. Arriving at the host's palatial estate, Nasruddin's stomach was rumbling, his mouth parched and dry, and he was looking forward to breaking his fast, but the guards, noting his bedraggled condition and sweat-stained clothes, ushered him to a corner a long distance away from the head table at which the mayor and other important townsfolk were seated.

The tables were laden with large platters of dates, pistachios, cashew nuts, dried fruits, olives, freshly made bread, piping hot dishes of falafel, kofte, kebabs, lamb and chicken pilaf, and an array of desserts—halva, date rolls, stewed figs, and baklava.

Scores of people, all dressed in their best, were already seated at the tables, tucking into the food, but nobody made room for Nasruddin, no one offered him anything to eat or drink and everyone behaved as if he wasn't even there. Deeply offended by the host's neglect and the other guests' behaviour and unable to enjoy his meal, Nasruddin decided to leave.

Hurrying home, he had a quick wash, changed into a magnificent embroidered coat and silk turban, and returned to the feast. This time the welcome he received was completely different—the guards bowed and showed him to a seat nearer the top table. The host greeted him warmly, and many of the townsfolk waved and beckoned to him from all corners of the room to sit with them.

Nasruddin sat down quietly. Picking up a handful of dates, he carefully placed them in his coat pocket, saying: 'Eat, coat, eat.' Next, he took a handful of nuts and put them into another pocket, repeating: 'Enjoy your meal, coat, eat your fill.' Grabbing handfuls of food, he shovelled some of it into his coat's pockets and rubbed the rest of it on his turban.

The guests seated around him stopped eating as they watched this strange behaviour. Everyone in the room was staring at Nasruddin, wondering what he was doing. The host hurried over. 'Nasruddin, what's the matter? Why are you putting food in your coat pocket

and rubbing it on your turban?'

'Well,' replied Nasruddin, 'when I first came to this banquet in my old work clothes, I was not welcome. No one would even speak to me. But, when I changed into this coat and turban, suddenly I was greeted warmly. So I realized it was not I that was welcome at this party, but my clothing. Therefore, I am feeding my coat and turban, making sure that they are well nourished and content, because without them I would have gone hungry.'

Teaching a Horse to Sing

During a visit to the capital, a small crowd gathered to hear Nasruddin's views on a variety of topics. A bystander called out: 'Mullah, do you think it is right that people should pay with their lives when the sultan embarks on military campaigns one after the other?'

'Whenever a monarch errs, it is his

people who pay the penalty,' Nasruddin replied.

Word of this jibe immediately reached Sultan Omar through his lackeys. Taking offence at the taunt, the sultan had Nasruddin arrested and imprisoned on charges of heresy and treason. Nasruddin apologized profusely and begged forgiveness, which made the sultan so angry that he decreed that Nasruddin should be beheaded the following day.

On the morning of his execution, Nasruddin made a final appeal. 'Your Lordship, may God grant you a long and healthy life! You have known me for many years and are aware that I am a great teacher. It will be a huge loss to your kingdom if I am executed and my vast reserves of knowledge die with me. I appeal to you most earnestly to delay my sentence for one year, during which time I will teach your favourite horse to sing.'

Sultan Omar did not believe that such a thing was possible, but his anger had cooled and he was amused by the audacity of Nasruddin's claim. 'Very well,' he said, 'I will grant your request. You can move into the stablemen's quarters right away but if at the end of the year you have not taught my horse to sing, believe me you will wish you had been executed today.'

When Nasruddin's friends visited him later that evening, they found him in high spirits, humming happily to himself. 'How can you be so cheerful?' they asked. 'Surely you do not believe that you can teach the sultan's horse to sing?'

'Maybe, maybe not,' Nasruddin replied. 'But now I have a whole year, which I did not have yesterday, and a lot can happen in that time. It is possible that the sultan might forgive me and order my release. It is possible that he could die in one of his frequent battles or succumb to illness. It is possible that the horse might die or I could die too. But I'm not going to lose heart. I've heard that in some western countries, people have managed

to teach horses to dance to music. So, if horses can dance, maybe this one can be taught to sing.'